The Darkest City
A Novella

Andrei Guruianu

Artwork by Teknari

ISBN-978-1-944388-08-9
Library of Congress Control Number: 2017947980

Fomite
58 Peru Street
Burlington, VT 05401
www.fomitepress.com

Contents

To the Reader

The Darkest City is a dialogue conducted in text and images between Romanian-born writer Andrei Guruianu and American photographer and visual artist Teknari. *The Darkest City* draws its inspiration from Teknari's black and white photographs of the Southern Tier of New York, whose small cities and villages have at times been labeled by some as "drive through" kind of places. Once known for being the birthplace of IBM, the Endicott Johnson shoe factories that furnished boots for American soldiers in WWII, Guglielmo Marconi's first radio tower, as well as the Twilight Zone series, large parts of the area now lie in disrepair, abandoned, a modern ruinscape. The claw marks are visible on the empty factories, boarded up storefronts, the houses and churches that have seen the rise and fall of industry. Despite the inevitable change and fresh coat of paint that comes with time, the image remains often dark and bleak, one that unfortunately is all too familiar when one conjures up visions of small town America.

And yet within the tension that forms in such places between past and present one curiously finds a resurgent spirit and a thriving arts scene, with dozens of artists setting up studios, galleries, and workshops throughout downtown areas among empty shops and vacant buildings. The paradox of economic stagnation and the artistic and cultural boom it engenders is at the heart of this manuscript, where the reader is asked to consider whether blight, the so-called "hard times", is a prerequisite for creation and creativity, or whether a more complex relationship exists between such places and the individual.

In many ways the tension at the heart of *The Darkest City* is one that plays out on a smaller scale in each of our daily lives. While we undoubtedly live in a digital culture of speed, brevity, and the now, we are nonetheless also a culture seemingly obsessed with a permanent sense of nostalgia, often for things, places, and times we have never experienced. When being hurled headlong into the future with each push of a button or swipe of the screen, there seems to be a very real need to have at least one foot planted in the past where, however murky the image, we might find something that resonates and serves as an anchor. As *The Darkest City* is rooted in the ancient practice of ekphrastic exchange and artistic dialogue, we invite readers along the way to contribute their thoughts and reflections and insert themselves into this narrative— be it on art and aesthetics, on memory and loss, or on identity and a sense of purpose and belonging. In the following pages we ask you to consider along with us: What do our modern lives—suspended between the metaphorical here and then—look like, and how do we go about living them to their fullest?

What interests me is the transformation, not the monument. I don't construct ruins, but I feel ruins are moments when things show themselves. A ruin is not a catastrophe. It is the moment when things can start again.

—Anselm Kiefer

Latitude, Longitude

Nothing ever happens in the darkest city. At least nothing that matters. Icarus drowns every day in its rivers and the fish turn a blind eye to the details, bury their noses in mud.

Actually, something almost happened once, or people mistakenly thought that it did, but the records were corrected soon after and the blunder is talked about now only by those who remember the day with a certain sense of wistfulness. It was a typically dark afternoon defined by the smallest burden of light. Nothing was happening, and indeed no one expected anything to happen. But for the purposes of illustrating what it looks like when we are misled into believing something has taken place, here is the scenario:

A mother pushing a stroller with a child inside is attempting to cross the street but she is doing so where the edge of the sidewalk doesn't quite meet at street level and there is a jolt, not exactly violent but it's enough; the child, not buckled into the stroller, falls out and lands on the ground and hits his head, or his knees, or both, that part is hardly relevant, but at this point he begins to cry, more like a wail, after which the mother picks him up and slams him back into the stroller, says "Sit down and shut up", and continues to cross to the other side of the street while the child's cries are muffled by distance.

~

In the darkest city there is a long-standing law against fooling around in cemeteries among tombstones. But in a place where even the stones are falling apart it is not uncommon for two people to get high and make love on the broken slabs out of sheer boredom. Some are falling apart themselves rather beautifully, hair and eye shadow and torn jeans of another era. Nostalgia in rags. Always another time. Some of them are simply lost, can't even think about a future life that they might never live; each day is everything and nothing. Some have known this their entire lives so they sleep together out of desperation, out of blind need that has all of the appearances of passion. But it's not that. Things happen out of passion, things that matter. But not here.

So when someone is caught, and inevitably they are, out of carelessness, stupidity, or outright disregard for anything sacred, the city makes a big deal out of it and calls it vandalism. They always want everything to mean something, to be of consequence, and don't understand that some things can simply be as inconsequential as two people wanting nothing more than to live. So the police are called, there is a fine, a slap on the wrist. A good talking to. Everyone eventually knows their names as the two who were caught fooling around on tombstones. Their names are easy to remember because it helps us forget our own. What no one ever asks is whose tombstone it was. How did they choose where to lie down? What name, what epitaph burned briefly on a bare back as they counted stars?

~

Even outside of the cemeteries the darkest city is a city of ghosts. Beer drinking ghosts, gambling ghosts, daytime-TV-watching ghosts, drug addicted ghosts, unborn ghosts, slit-your-throat-for-a-pint sort of ghosts, you get the idea. A dead city needs a good number of the dead to be just barely alive to be counted when the census comes around. They prop up the broken awnings, they lean against guardrails and bar counters at noon, they haunt the places where everything barely exists.

The rooming houses are full of them. The abandoned factories are full of them. Even the workshop floors still echo with their footsteps. On a quiet night you can hear the machines, the gun-like staccato, the sound of a man clearing his throat as he looks around for the boss then down to the ground and spits. At home maybe he chooses to end it all, maybe it has already ended. What he cares about is that when he wanted to spit he was free to spit and he did so, and it felt as good as few things ever do.

~

Depending on whom you ask you will hear many different stories about how the darkest city got its name. Some are humorous, some make obscure references to the long dead and famous, some to an act of God. But stories always try to hide something. That's the point of a story. And the storytellers are no better. They are weak and they want attention, validation that living through it and suffering through it had been worth it.

What you won't find here is anyone arguing about the fact that the darkest city is dark. I heard a man say that once at a roadside bar as bleak as its name. He was nursing a beer. It was likely the only honest thing to ever be said in the darkest city. What people happened to be there simply nodded and that's how you knew it was true. I just kept watching him as he turned his beer on the counter, as the glass groaned against the wood, an already somber sky above turning black.

~

Because the darkest city did away with history books

years ago it is difficult to confirm any one myth of its name. The books were always the same, year after year, an anthology of names and numbers, until someone on the city council finally asked, "What's the point of history if it never changes?" And since nothing ever happens in the darkest city then naturally nothing ever changes, making the point of a history moot. The past, present, and future are now all lumped into one, a perpetual *remember when*. Has happened, is happening, and will happen all refer to the same thing, which, grammatically speaking is impossible, but historically speaking it could be understood as the life of a photograph that never *is* and always *has been*.

~

A place without history also has no beginning or end, which theoretically makes it impossible to get lost. Which, of course, means everyone is lost in their own way, unable to get attached to anything, to get one's bearings in space or in time.

An unintended consequence is that without a beginning
or end asking for directions is useless, and giving
directions is even more so. In the darkest city old men
could be seen on their porches killing time, just waiting
for someone to stop and ask them how to get from point
A to point B. Most wait their whole lives to be asked this
simple question and never get the chance to answer. A
few are luckier than the others and—having practiced
for years the art of not knowing—shrug their shoulders
with remarkable artistry.

~

Believe what part of this you will, was how I heard
about it the first time, and to this day I'm not sure if it

is merely hearsay or legend or ingrained as truth in the collective consciousness of the place, something like a blur in the corner of the eye, the vague contour of what may or may not actually be there.

So, believe what part of this you will: Generations ago, which is a rough estimate as such things usually go, it was decided by a nearly unanimous vote that all those living in the darkest city would lead dark lives. The one dissenting voice was beaten until he couldn't see anymore. If you live outside of the darkest city that's what the history books say. To illustrate the point, in the books there are a couple of photographs of electrical wires and vacant lots. They are labeled as Fig. 1 and Fig. 3. In between there is blank space and the children are all encouraged to guess and draw their own Fig. 2's right onto the pages. They love that part of the lesson!

Naturally it's a trick—you can't draw emptiness— but the kids don't learn about it until much later. Some never do. Meanwhile crude pictures of the darkest city hang from magnets in kitchens all over the world; in the corner the smudge of a stamp, or gold star as proof that the child has indeed got it all figured out.

~

In a show of normality or sheer marketing genius, there is a combination visitor center and gift shop located just off the main highway overpass that runs up along the city's eastern flank and continues north. Almost everyone continues north. But those who do stop usually make a point to pick up something at the gift shop. The most popular item is the all black teddy bear wearing a black t-shirt with "Someone in The Darkest

City Loves You" embroidered across the chest. Second is the snow globe with black snow, The Darkest City dark chocolate collector's tin, and of course the "I Like My Coffee the Same Way I Like My City—Dark" coffee mug. The shop is open from 9 a.m. to 5 p.m. Monday through Saturday. On Sundays the main room doubles as a banquet hall for corporate functions and weddings.

Conspicuously absent from the visitor center's litany of brochures (two, to be exact, the rest of the wooden slots filled with Chinese takeout menus, an undertaker's flyer, and a circular for the nearby supermarket where all of the offers have already expired), is any mention of the number of telephone and electrical wires suspended above and crisscrossing the darkest city. If you sit still and listen hard enough on a quiet summer evening some say you might still be able to hear Marconi's echo radiating from one of the central towers. From there the voice frays and splits and dissipates through the cables along with hundreds of other voices that had something to say once, begun a sentence with conviction then reconsidered, stopped midway and seemed to ponder over a great thought, an epiphany, but in reality it was probably much simpler and more ordinary than that.

~

As would be expected, there is no shortage of churches in the darkest city. Sometimes the candles lit in memory of the dead and the living serve as the only light for days on end. But each church had wanted to be the first and that led over time to animosity, outright hatred and violence by otherwise good men and women, not to mention the little kids who, upon learning that they might not be the first, indeed possibly second, third, or even last, would throw temper tantrums and could not be appeased with the sweetest indulgences.

In what is remembered now as a miracle, an immaculate act of governance, one particularly inspired mayor, mostly because he hated the sound of whiny children, passed legislation mandating that all churches from then on would be called The Darkest Church. All of the children applauded. To differentiate among the churches one simply would add its location, for example The Darkest Church on Broad Street or The Darkest Church on Main Avenue. What was undoubtedly an act of sheer brilliance and outstanding leadership is instead now attributed to an obscure interpretation of the scriptures, which, if you're clever enough, can be made to say just about anything.

Monochrome Dreams, Pt. I

*T*here's not that many of the good ones left, they'll tell you. At the entrance to the last movie theater still standing, one of them is begging for change. He remembers, and for a while longer everyone who sees him remembers too. But no one says so. That would mean admitting that whatever it is isn't any longer and it's never coming back, and what good is memory without a single prayer that one might someday see it come to pass again? That's all that the good ones are good for—blind promise, blind faith, maybe proof that in a lifetime you can make some mistakes and still be called kind and decent.

The doors close and the bargain flick starts, seats nearly empty, and for two hours everyone is tucked small into a narrow portion of a different world. It smells and sounds like a different world.

Those who fall in love in the darkest city—against their better judgment and well-meaning advice from those who've been wrong enough times to know a thing or two—set themselves up for disappointment. They work hard at love, they do their best to love, but it just doesn't add up. The problem is that they look outside of themselves and want to see the accumulation of that struggle, a stacking up of the small gestures made with honest effort. They look and it just doesn't amount to something visible, some tangible proof that it has made any real difference. And the truth is that it hasn't. It never has. They say "I've tried, I gave it a shot, and for what? Nothing happened." Of course nothing did. Where has proof of love ever existed without a single doubt? Should they know enough to look inward the answer might be different, but more likely it will still leave them unhappy, a part of them always unsatisfied. They know that's not how the story is supposed to turn out—with some kind of moral about limits and regret—so they go on trying to love, which I suppose is better than trying nothing at all.

~

The landscape: hills and rivers and rock. That's really what makes a place breathe, what makes it heave

and sigh and shudder, what makes you understand its
motives. It's what gives you the pleasant views, if there
are any, and the dotted trenches of its valleys, if it has
any, the things it hides or throws out into the open for all
to see. The weather, too, is dependent on the landscape,
which only by chance ever differs from one day to the
next.

~

There used to be a railway station in the darkest city,
and trains used to pass through with coal and gas and
grain. Like most things it shut down long ago, but
the silver rails still cut beautiful lines of coming and
going deep through the valley and the freight trains
move through at a steady pace. You can hear them
in the distance, the steel wheels on rail echoing off
the hills, the sound seeming that much farther away,

impossibly far, so that you begin to doubt what it is, if you've heard anything at all. Like a second-hand story passed down until it has gotten so far from itself you can't even begin to guess how it started. In those moments all you can do is trust what you know—and you know the trains pass through here, you know that distance can be misleading.

~

As dusk falls in the darkest city it does so with a subtle likeness to a grainy black and white window through which the other side is admired with a mix of curiosity and hesitation. One hand is pressed up against the glass, the other one grasps the familiar contours of the room. This is all that one is capable of at times, all that one can do when faced with a question mark fashioned from circumstances that offer nothing but false choice.

Then, on days after, everything in the darkest city appears as if frozen to a dead stop in one long exposure. The ghosts multiply, expand, stretch to their limits, the nearly dead suspended in the cobwebs of a blur. A string of lights turns men and women into monochrome marionettes, turns the steel and mortar grid into a cardboard city, a lonely playground set, an abandoned field made for the kind of flowers that only grow through the cracks. They have no names. They are the flowers that grow in the gaps.

As the morning haze lifts you rub your eyes and blink to get a better view; and it is a better view; and everything looks the same. But it has gotten a little bit warmer, the shapes softened and more pleasant to the eye, to the imagined touch, and you can't help but wonder if, in time, you might even get used to this.

~

Getting used to it, turning to habit. County fairs and homecoming games. The parades where all of the children come out to see the fire trucks and the vintage Ford pickups roll on by. Also the circus, they all talk about the circus. It comes through twice a year and it is always sold out—once after Christ has risen (the weather is good on the animals then) and once in early December (the weather isn't as good then but neither are the men good to animals most of the time). Everyone goes and they each have a favorite: the high wire act, the lions, the horse riding monkey, not the clowns, never the sad-faced clowns, the acrobats, the fire eaters, etc. And yet every year there is one seat that remains empty. The seat is sold, bought and paid for, but no one ever sits there. Instead there's someone somewhere at a kitchen table saying, "One fewer. It's not much, but it's something."

At night, after the last show has ended and everyone has gone home, a young acrobat, yet to get his wings and fly above the crowd, climbs to where the empty seat had been. He sits there for a long time in silence, looking down at the circus floor, finally asking no one in particular, given all he knows now, *Is it still acceptable to dream?*

~

There isn't a single person here who hasn't lost something. It's so common in fact that a typical morning greeting has become "What have you lost since yesterday?" It is much more considerate than the overused "What did you do yesterday?" because it automatically implies a certain degree of sensitivity to one's plight, whereas the latter confers no special intention upon the question aside from its habitual and disingenuous nature. What have you lost? The answers vary anywhere from earrings to wallets to keys and small animals, to the intangible, such as sleep, energy, motivation. The most common answer is hope, and those who ask always dread hearing it. You cannot simply brush it off with the usual, "Oh, don't worry, it will turn up soon."

~

And so every day the people here take inventory of themselves. They count their two eyes, two arms, two legs, and so on. Tattoos of names, birthdays, horoscope signs, some kind of record, a point of referral, something solid to keep coming back to. One needs to know what to rely on when heading out the door. Some days it's worse than others and it means one needs to be reminded of the missing limb or a missing tooth or a limp that wasn't there the day before, but even then it's better knowing what not to count on.

That's how a day is measured in the darkest city—what you can't count on any longer. The obvious isn't even counted anymore in the inventory: jobs, money, pride, etc. You don't need those things to get by. Instead girls and boys are out on front steps tossing stones, starting rumors, turning fantasy into fact, enumerating dreams already dreamt into oblivion. But as long as one hand reaches out for another and finds a shred of warmth they'll make of it much more than it is; and in the darkest city every little bit counts, even the naked lies told with a straight face over the open mouth of a beer can.

~

It should come as no surprise then that a good part of the population of the darkest city is employed in what is now mostly a dying profession, creating their own monsters so they have something to destroy. The pay is miserable but as all works of love go they do it out of a perverse sort of pleasure reserved for the insane or the irreparably broken hearted. You would think they would instead work on mending their broken hearts, but the broken pieces hold together enough to not fall apart.

This is why what you will never hear is people tell you that they are sad, depressed, or lonely. They'll say *I'm bored* or *I'm tired* or *I don't know*, which is close to the same thing. So they go on building the absurd out of scraps and discarded objects, out of nails and planks of wood, anything that will put up a good fight.

One night I met a woman in the darkest city whom no one really knows, at least knows nothing about who she is or isn't, except the fact that she has truly beautiful eyes. They agree on that, but if you press them on it they can't really explain why except to say that they know they're much more than pretty. Something about the word doesn't fit, the same way that *bored* or *tired* doesn't quite cut it and everyone knows what the real answer is. She was beautiful then, we'll have to settle on that, and the city that night was especially dark, one thing collapsed into another, indistinguishable. That's certainly something that a word like pretty isn't made for.

~

Out of nowhere—nonsense, gibberish, perfectly so: *I'm just fine with dressing from Goodwill, you know what I mean? Yard sales and thrift shops, Tuesday sales at the Salvation Army. Gotta get there early though. Learned that the hard way.* That's how she began the conversation. I'd asked her, *Aren't you cold?* We were standing at a bus stop, she had no jacket, it was cold out. I had the feeling that she was trying to sell me something but even she wasn't sure what. She kept averting her eyes, she would not let them do the talking. When the bus came I got on and she stayed behind, still selling something, her hands now buried deep in her pockets.

Don't trust boys whose names start with the letter J, she said the next time we ran into each other—bus stop again. Small time, small talk, temporary. The first name that came to mind when she said that was Jesus—though I know she had in mind someone who'd jilted her, who'd broken her heart, who'd stolen her lunch money, who kissed and told, who didn't keep promises. But all I could think about was Jesus, what does it mean to have faith and then lose it, who or what suffers our blame?

An Incomplete Answer

Hang around a place long enough as much as I have and you start asking a lot of *how's* and *why's*. It's nothing more than curiosity getting the best of you—it wouldn't solve anything, wouldn't change the lived-in feel of each day, of each hour. But you look around and you have counted the streetlights, the stop signs, the crack houses, the broken boarded up windows, the weekly gatherings at the VFW, how many people ride bicycles on the sidewalk, how many dropouts eviscerate cigars on park benches during school hours.

Then at some point you run out of facts. Or maybe you've run out of ways to count them differently each time. All that you are left with are questions. When that happens the one suggestion you're sure to get is to go see the man who has not finished anything in years; or, as he is most commonly referred to, the "Once he could have..." artist of the darkest city.

~

I wanted to know, what does it mean to be indebted to the past? So much so that you cannot leave it behind, that it hounds your every step, follows you home, watches over you as you sit down for dinner, as you take your last wakeful breath every night? In every city you will find this, an inability to let go, to fully break off and dwell in the present. Enclaves of the past they're called, pockets of brownstones, entire neighborhoods as colonies of the dead—streets named after famous authors or presidents or classical composers. Their names cling to the eaves of concert halls, bandstands, parks, picnic tables, wedding gazebos, crooked benches, decrepit tennis courts, sidewalk planters, a whole world living *in memoriam.* At night I imagine the dead doing more living than we ever do—Brahms head-butting Hamilton for some misunderstanding over the word "revolutionary"—*Du bist voller Scheiße,* you could hear him say—while Goethe and Twain are busy pranking Hemingway, drunk out of his mind and knocking on strange doors looking for one good bottle of wine. They can do that and still we build them roads, the same ones we walk for hours just so we'll get back to where we left.

~

The first time I met the artist I was walking up the stairs to his studio just as the blur of a figure was storming out of the place, confused, frustrated, in a hurry, all possible, all with their own explanations that I would never get from him. Through the open doorway the artist could be seen lighting a cigarette, looking up through the first breath of smoke as he spotted me. *The strange ones have a way of finding me,* he said in my direction, after which naturally I hesitated to give him my name.

~

The strange ones. I couldn't get that image out of my head. They were at my heels afterward for days. Whom do you trust in a place where the words of God and of the junkie prophet jostle for territory? One works to build bridges, the other to burn them. Both peddle in fear and both have laid out their virtues on Main Street among addicts and the homeless, high school jocks and the dime-a-dozen wannabe rockstars. They are professional hustlers, handing out flyers for that personal touch and business cards printed on at least 10% recycled—we're talking ethics and compassion after all, something that can hold its own next to the picture of a missing dog taped to a light post.

But when the summer storms come, as early as May, the paper is flayed, the ink pours into the gutter. And in the middle of a downpour the streets are empty, the shops have closed early, everyone is gone. For a moment you consider running. For how long? Where? You consider alternatives, always *what ifs*. The papers say nothing about this, neither do the poor missing animals soaked to the bone. In such moments take the only option you're given—look at the sky and think about the indifference of rain. How happy it looks to be falling.

~

The day after a good rain is one of the most pleasant times in the darkest city. For a couple of hours the silence and the stillness speak to the birds and they speak back, breaking into wind-borne color and streaks of gray. This is the only place they've ever called home, where they build their nests out of whatever they might find, where they leave only to play homage to the life of a bird—roaming, drifting, flight seemingly without purpose—in the end turning their eyes to the north, the cold that comes always too early.

~

The artist didn't know much at all, despite what everyone seemed to think. They tell you of the many things he had accomplished, direct you here and there all over the city to see them, but I never found one thing of importance. We struck up a friendship over silence. He liked to invite me over for beer on summer evenings, especially if I offered to bring the beer. He liked to go around his studio hugging a bottle close to his chest while stopping in front of some project in progress and study it with a lover's eyes, with the eyes of a boy in love for the first time. And I genuinely felt that he was in love, but exactly what it is that he loved I'm not sure even he could tell you.

~

As soon as I can I'm leaving this place. There's not a

single person that has not uttered this phrase at least once in the darkest city. Of course, there are many varieties, such as, *When I have enough money I'll...*, and *If only I had the chance..."*, and so on. Where will you go? I ask. *Anywhere. Anywhere but here.* That never changes.

On some days I find myself walking down to the river where I can spend an entire afternoon face to face with the water. Two rivers, to be precise. I stand at the confluence of bodies of water, one body slamming itself into the other then rushing on downstream as if it had never happened. Where I stand only the mud remains churning, there is nothing you can see below; above, the sun is blinding. The fish do not know the names of the rivers. They do not know of the river the way you and I do.

~

I have to confess that I find it easier to talk to the barflies here. Their lies are more honest. All of the other men and women have too much to hide when they come together at night. Some say they have nothing left but a vague sense of self. *What am I if*

I can't... ? Who am I if I'm not... ? But everyone is hiding something, in the beauty parlors and the nail salons, the massage parlors and the neon colored bar dives where they go to see who's still standing at the end of a long day.

~

The artist says that's even more reason to make something new again, to build it if you must out of bit of torn leather and wood and spit-shine. But his studio was always empty as far as I could tell, his tools piled on a table in the corner, only a broken figure somewhat in his likelness half-penned onto a life-size sheet of paper. He would stand there in front of it, as if pleading, as if in supplication, wonderment, wanting answers, and at last he would speak to it—*I know, I know.* After which he seemed to be done, to have finished his day's work.

~

Advice you're likely to hear from an old man who no longer gives a damn during a cigarette break on bingo night: *Look, if you think God has something planned for you that doesn't mean you just sit around and wait for it. Sometimes you have to just take that leap and do something. Just in case God doesn't really have something planned for everyone. I mean, how could he? There's so many of us and he'd get the plans mixed up and that would lead to a lot of pissed off people. But you can take your chances if you don't believe me, like all the others. Just sit around and wait. It works for some I guess.*

~

This morning I stand with coffee in hand and watch from the same dusty window as the fog moves in, as I tell myself that I need to get away from myself. And maybe that's why I came here, far away but never far enough. When I turn on my heels I'm back to where I started.

Monochrome Dreams, Pt. II

The artist hadn't left his apartment in days. *It's all here*, he said looking down into the palms of his hands. I looked where his eyes led me but I saw nothing.

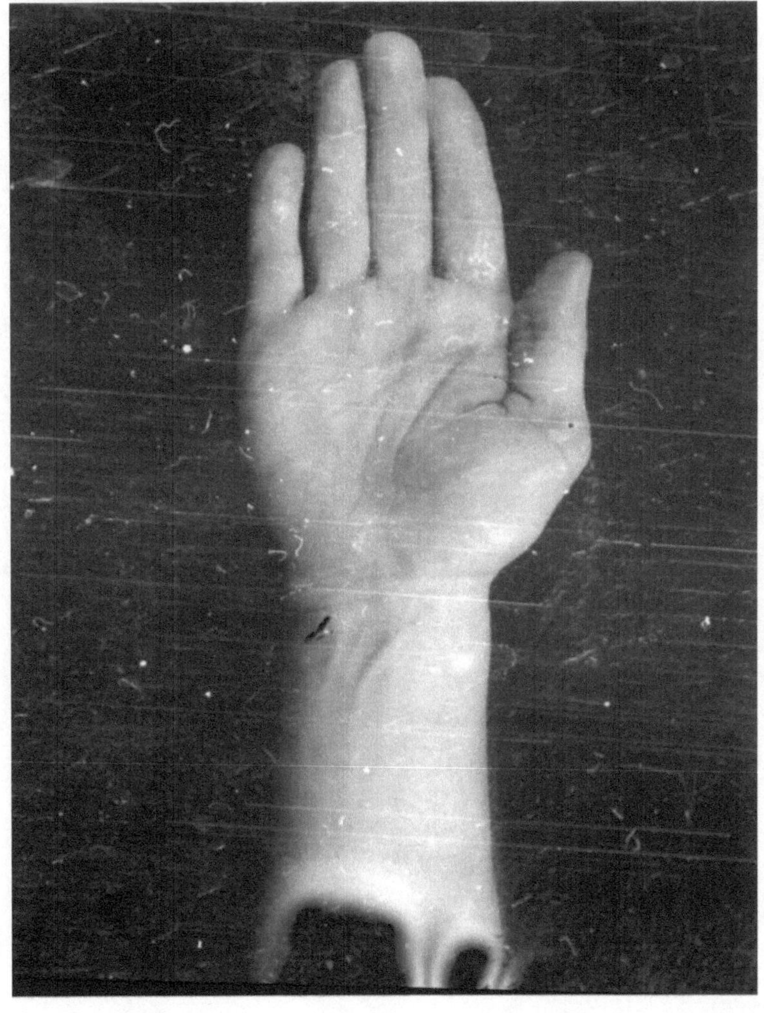

~

Given enough time the sense of despair crawls into even the most intimate places. Into the dense fabric of it. It turns everything black as night. And in the dark you're free to imagine how the whole world tonight is fucking on a really tight schedule. How the plates and forks are in the sink left to soak until morning. How some people have the luxury to never think of these things.

~

But I'm at the point where I no longer get upset at the clouds for taking their time rolling in. I listen to the wind marching ahead, the birds changing their tone, the stones reflecting their ambivalence to it. I think about a line that would capture all this beautifully and simply. I think of getting it tattooed on my body, somewhere only I could see it and know that it's true.

~

As I get home late one evening the widow who rents the room below me is in the doorway unlacing her boots.

She leaves all of her shoes lined up at the door. She sweeps her few feet of cement, has a doormat that says *Welcome Friends.*

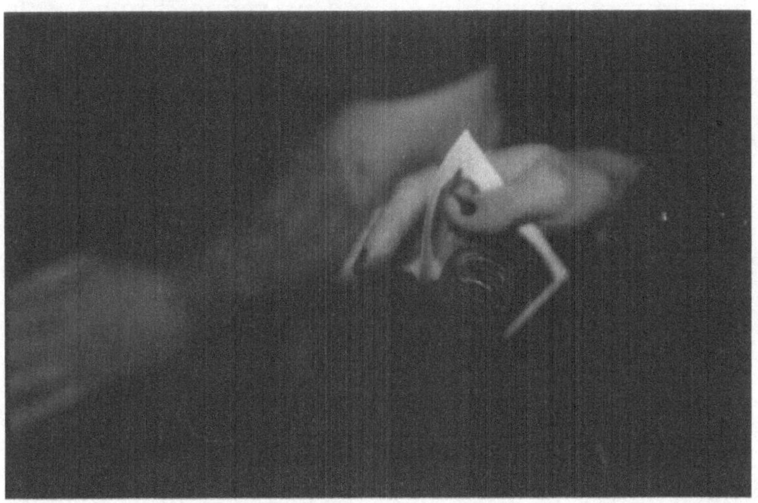

We stand for a moment in the hallway and before she turns to the door she says, *It was a good night tonight. I got a compliment on my boots.* What do you say to that? *That's great? I'm happy for you?* I didn't think that much of her boots. But people do think about these things, even stop and go out of their way to say something to someone else about these things. And maybe that is the only kind thing one person shares with another in the course of an entire day, a week, maybe one lonely month. Maybe that's all that a person needs to feel the full measure of themselves, to walk out the door onto the sidewalk with some stranger calling out through whiskey breath something negligible about footwear—which could mean nothing at all or it could mean everything in the world. After all it's just a word, but after a few drinks no one is really thinking about linguistics and signifiers or Nietzsche or God. More like how in the end we always end up reduced to a single word, reducing others with a single word, burying them, if we're lucky not to get buried ourselves.

Lucky, what it ultimately comes down to—how many here have wished for their luck to change—how many in the morning count their blessings that for now, at least, they're not on the losing end of an equation whose answer is *zero*?

~

At the diner over coffee and eggs and bread with too much butter the artist and I were talking about making art and making love, and I can't remember exactly which one of the two we settled on as being more important for happiness but there was certainly some overlap.

We ate like two men not thinking about eating. But there were the sounds of the fork and knife, and the booth across from us where everyone had a bland face and the conversation was lifeless and dull, something about car repairs and life insurance and the traffic in this town.

Outside the sun was standing on its head on the corner waiting for the light to change. The waitress was doing her job but she wasn't into it at all, not the way some of them can fake it sweetly with *How are ya, Honey?* or *What'll it be, Doll?* I looked at her then looked back at the sun and I thought that they're both just doing their jobs waiting for the end of the day, for when it's time to make some room between who you are and who you imagine you might be.

We finished our food and kept talking art and love, and one must certainly have won out over the other but we can't agree now on which one it was. To this day I still want to know. I'm upset with myself that I always must know.

~

Lately I've begun to dream in black and white. In my dreams I make black&white love, I have black&white hopes and black&white fears. Much of them are in silence, much of them spent watching myself from a distance. But how simple everything is in those dreams, how easy the choice to be made when faced with a fork in the road.

~

One day the artist confessed to me, and it was the most he'd ever spoken since we'd known each other, the most he would ever speak after:

I remember my bedroom door in the apartment where I grew up covered with stickers and pictures torn from comic books and magazines of perfect men and women and superheroes, but back then the impossible didn't seem quite so distant as it does now when I stare at the white wall and the even whiter ceiling and wonder how it is possible to think about making love, making anything meaningful when the first thing I want to do is get up and leave, let go of everything, just let it drift as far as it will. Or, if that's not really an option, then I just want to sit at the window with a pint of whiskey until it gets dark and the stars are out mysterious and beautiful, which feels at least like some kind of justice, maybe a small miracle, over there over the hill, where the clock is a full hour ahead and we're not already dead.

Almost Right

Instructions for writing a postcard from the darkest city:

You are here and the weather is either pleasant or otherwise, but you must make a brief note of it. You don't want to write about it but you do. They will ask. The city fits into gaps of a tattered story. You can't remember what else needs to be filled but something does. Something is missing. It is lacking. You write, *Wish you were...*, but then stop and put a line though it. A small doubt if you mean it. You wonder if you chose the right picture to go with the sentiment. Skyline, river, monument. Would it change anything? Would they know what you're really thinking? You have so many doubts but there's no room on the postcard. You never write the postcard.

~

Almost a year has passed, which, if I could be honest, I never thought would happen. At least that was never the plan. Forget fortunetellers—I'll take old men on bingo nights every time!

The first signs of winter. Miserable roads. Everyone begins cursing as if it were the first time. All talk turns to the weather and they all agree, *Ah, yes, it's going to be a long one, a hard, lingering winter.*

~

In the streets the children of the darkest city fight imaginary wars like all of the children before them and all of the children to come. Death and resurrection in the shadow of abandoned factories. Just ordinary miracles easily forgotten with a fresh change of clothes. When you ask any of them what they did all day, the answer is always *Nothing*, which is as honest as they will ever be, as any of us ever have been. They are not unhappy.

~

There are not many walls in the darkest city, nothing you could climb over, break down, put your weight against; only dead end roads, endless roads, no outlet signs. It is easy to feel trapped in open space.

~

In the garden next door the plaster Mary and Joseph kneel in the dirt praying. The snowdrift is nearly as tall as they are. At times all you can see are the two severed heads over a rim of snow— split from the body and floating, all smiles.

~

With the cold winds settling in from the north I began to spend more time with the artist. I'd show up in the morning and watch him work through the day. He didn't mind. Sometimes he barely noticed I was there.

What do you think is the secret to making art? he asked once. *I don't know, inspiration, I guess, talent,* I said.

No, it's all about the line, he said. Everything divides itself to one side or the other of a line. Bend it and everything bends around it. Nothing is more powerful than a single line. And he took some photographs from a stack on the table and he arranged them in lines whose logic only he knew before scattering them again. The more he worked the more questions I had.

~

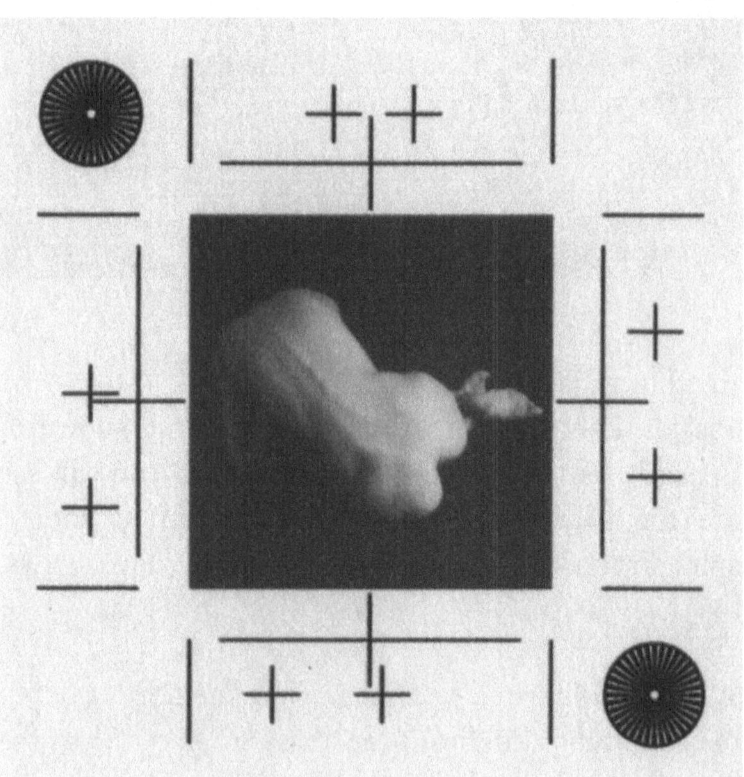

What bothers me now, looking back, is not so much that I had too many questions to ask, but that I had the urge to ask them. My whole life I felt that having an answer would mean something. But you don't ask a man bent over by the yoke of his days *Why?* just to sooth your own curiosity. You ask how you might make the weight easier to bear. Or at least have the dignity to look away and swallow your guilt, leave things to be decided one way or another.

The artist never asked any questions. Nothing that would weigh you down. And he rarely said what he should have, but maybe in retrospect I'm projecting things, maybe it's just what I wanted him to do, to come right out and say it.

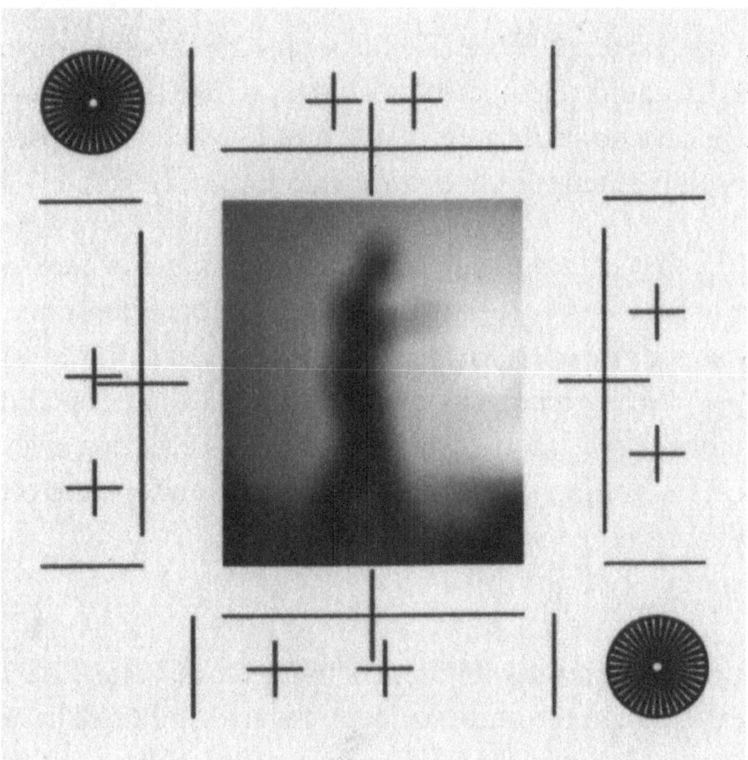

~

In a moment of madness or lucidity or both, Woolf
wrote once in her diaries, "How many times have people
used a pen or a paintbrush because they couldn't pull
the trigger?"

~

My question: *What do you do when you have neither
pen nor paintbrush?* The river, I imagine she might
say, you go to the river and you wait. *How long can
you wait?*

~

Living and not living take the same amount of courage.
But we don't celebrate those who choose the latter freely—
we have no medals for that sort of freedom. It exposes
us; it frightens us out of the comfort of conviction.

The fact is that one doesn't choose so much where to
live but where to die, for in each city you have died once,
many times over, each day closer to the end. But most
people can't handle living like that so they pick up and
move, they grab their things and run, as if getting away
means getting away from yourself, means heading off
death a little while longer.

~

And that's mostly all there is to my story. I was lost. I
ended up in the darkest city by chance. And I still have
questions about that, still too many questions, but I've

56

learned to get by without all of the answers.

Like I said, I was lost—and whatever that means to you will have to suffice—so I picked up the tattered ends of one life and traded it for another. Only when you have no sense of where you're going can you find a place like this that doesn't ask and doesn't care.

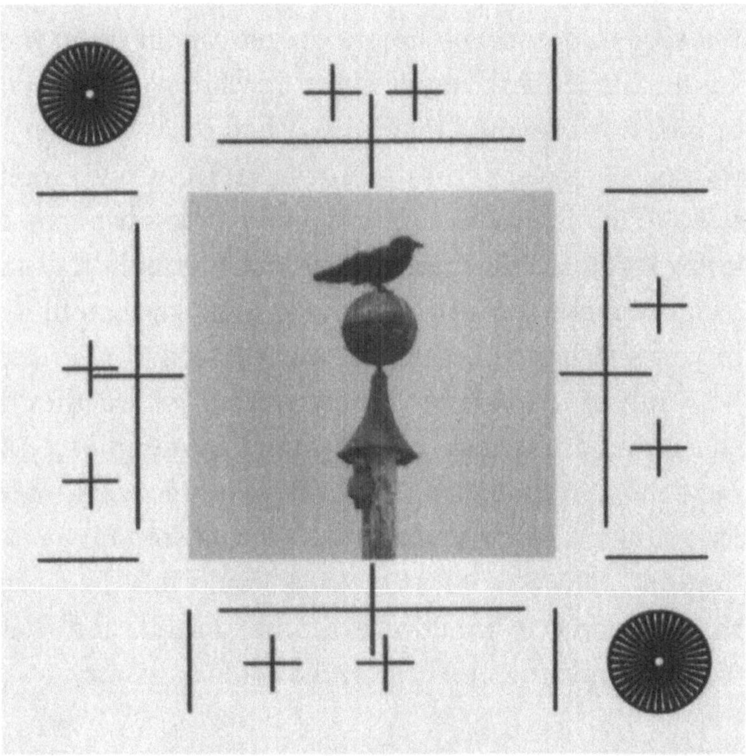

But you don't forget. And nothing in the darkest city is ever forgotten either. Even when there is not much to remember you feed on the smallest crumb of time you find tucked in your pocket, in the creases of a broken down shop coat, in the folds of an eye half open to the dawn. To forget such nothings would mean to erase yourself, to scrub clean what others would never consider mourning, that outline in the river's shore that is unmistakably you, in spite of what the waters have done.

~

It's easy to dream too much. To get caught up in the wind-sails of a myth and want to go wherever the good or bad storms would take you. When I was younger I wanted to travel across the country from one small town to another with only a typewriter to my name. I know it sounds saccharine now, but I thought that in order to make something you had to make something of yourself first and the best way to do that is to see how others had done it before you, where they'd succeeded and where they'd failed, come up just an inch short of the mark. With the weather at my back I would wander from place to place and stop for a few days in each to write its story. I would tell the story that no one else would ever bother to tell, and that would be my line notched on the walls of history.

But I didn't get too far. Rather I didn't see the need to get too much farther. What difference would it have made? One dream borrows from another the way myth traces its roots through the centuries to the first story chipped into the sides of cliff. You can still read it now if you look past all of the clutter; and you can hear it, too, it sounds as if the place is just clearing its throat. And so you clear your throat because it feels right, because you've got something lodged in there that needs to come out. But then you look around and everyone else is clearing their throat, never quite managing to get out what was so important to say.

~

Sometimes I bring my typewriter with me when I go to see the artist. It's only a black heap of metal and plastic, some cheap replica, but it mimics the hum of being alive and charged, cranked up ready to punch daylight in the teeth. Energy, verve, that's what was missing, I realized, and I say this to the artist as I lean over the keys, my hands poised, waiting for the word.

No, that kind of thinking won't be of any use to you here, he says casually, assured, in a voice that has its back to the world. *Neither will the books you have read, those even less so—they will not help with what you didn't know then; once it has passed all you can do is look back. The same for the books you will read a day or a year from now—they will not help you live with yourself today.* That voice again, as if it had turned already away from its latest proclamation, abandoned it and walked away, eyes to faraway corners and the soft streaks on a yet to be built horizon.

Then a pause, the kind of moment when silence is the only response that would fit. I look around the studio, a cluster of tools, tables full of brushes, clippings, film containers, a broken bird of an easel. He's finished nothing. He's made nothing you could put a name to, not a single thing you would say actually matters, and he sees in my silence that's exactly what I'm thinking. He sees I don't know how to begin writing about that.

It's all there is, he says as he looks down into the palms of his hands. And I look down too, we look together, but I see only the cracked lines carved into the lakebed of his soiled palms. I tell him this; he says that I'm almost right. He goes back to his work.

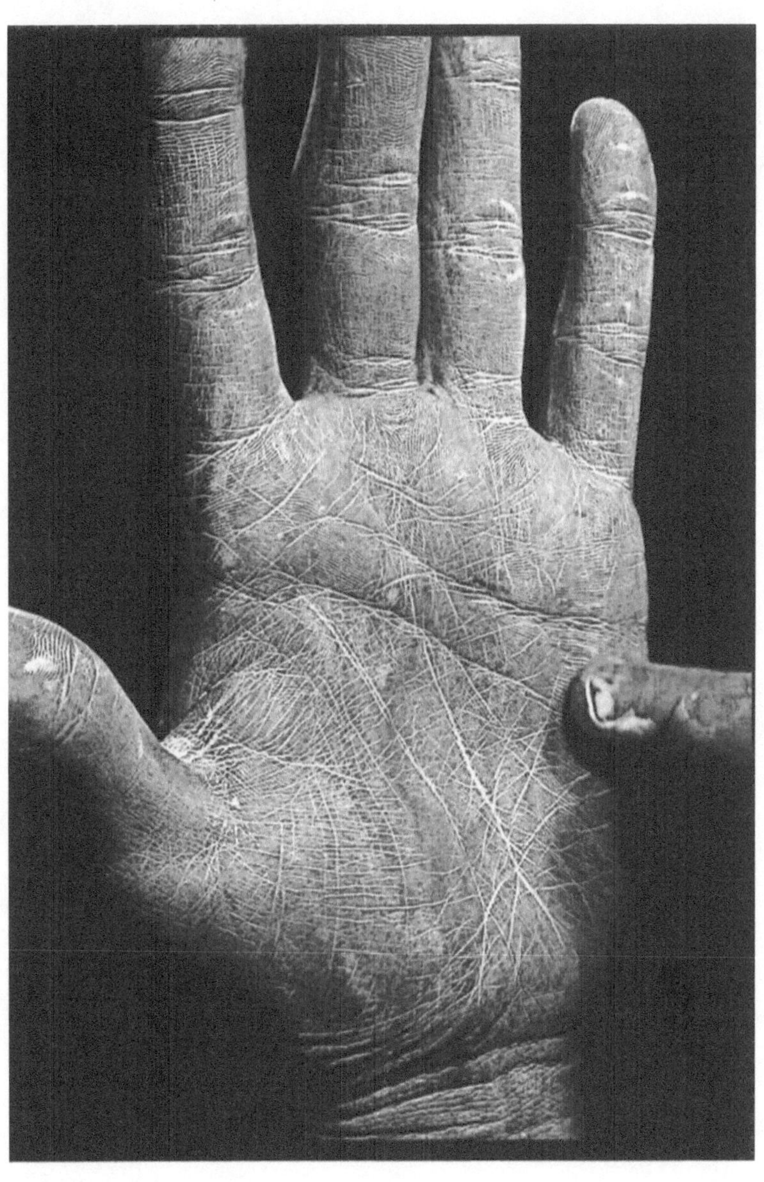

A Note on the Artwork

The photographs in *The Darkest City* were shot using homemade black and white film that Teknari creates in his own studio and leaves purposefully "unpolished". The chemicals are applied to the filmstrip unevenly, almost haphazardly, creating rough spots and gaps in the finished product. He then proceeds to shoot entire rolls of purposefully distressed film, never knowing exactly what the results will be. By surrendering a degree of artistic control to the mechanics of the process itself, entire shots and even film rolls might be ruined, with subjects blotted out or cut off by the placement of the film surface's random alignment. And sometimes, by sheer chance or accident, the subject in a certain frame will align with the contours within the film itself in such a way as to complement one another, to create an image that could not have been conceived through artistic vision alone. In such work, the altered medium meets common, ordinary content, forcing the viewer into a new language required to engage with and make sense of the final product—not unlike a surrealist painting that conjures a more fluid and malleable language of the imagination.

Authors

Andrei Guruianu is a Romanian-born writer and professor of writing. The author of more than a dozen books of poetry and prose, his works often explore such topics as memory and forgetting, the role of art and of the artist, and the ability of place to shape personal and collective histories. He currently teaches in the Expository Writing Program at New York University.

www.andreiguruianu.com

Teknari is a Binghamton, NY-based artist whose recent photographic and digital works explore the potential of chance and random occurrence to add nuance and depth to personal expression through the use of his own handmade silver gelatin emulsion film. He believes that despite the full presence of the artist in the process, photography is a subconscious effort on the part of both photographer and model, becoming ultimately an act of liberation from the confines of convention.

www.teknari.com

Fomite

About Fomite

A fomite is a medium capable of transmitting infectious organisms from one individual to another.

"The activity of art is based on the capacity of people to be infected by the feelings of others." Tolstoy, *What Is Art?*

Writing a review on Amazon, Good Reads, Shelfari, Library Thing or other social media sites for readers will help the progress of independent publishing. To submit a review, go to the book page on any of the sites and follow the links for reviews. Books from independent presses rely on reader to reader communications.

For more information or to order any of our books, visit
http://www.fomitepress.com/FOMITE/Our_Books.html

More Titles from Fomite...

Novels

Joshua Amses — *During This, Our Nadir*
Joshua Amses — *Raven or Crow*
Joshua Amses — *The Moment Before an Injury*
Jaysinh Birjepatel — *The Good Muslim of Jackson Heights*
Jaysinh Birjepatel — *Nothing Beside Remains*
David Brizer — *Victor Rand*
Paula Closson Buck — *Summer on the Cold War Planet*
Roger Coleman — *Skywreck Afternoons*
Marc Estrin — *Hyde*
Marc Estrin — *Kafka's Roach*
Marc Estrin — *Speckled Vanitie*
Zdravka Evtimova — *In the Town of Joy and Peace*
Zdravka Evtimova — *Sinfonia Bulgarica*
Daniel Forbes — *Derail This Train Wreck*
Greg Guma — *Dons of Time*

Fomite

Richard Hawley — *The Three Lives of Jonathan Force*
Lamar Herrin — *Father Figure*
Ron Jacobs — *All the Sinners Saints*
Ron Jacobs — *Short Order Frame Up*
Ron Jacobs — *The Co-conspirator's Tale*
Scott Archer Jones — *A Rising Tide of People Swept Away*
Maggie Kast — *A Free Unsullied Land*
Darrell Kastin — *Shadowboxing with Bukowski*
Coleen Kearon — *Feminist on Fire*
Coleen Kearon — *#triggerwarning*
Jan Englis Leary — *Thicker Than Blood*
Diane Lefer — *Confessions of a Carnivore*
Rob Lenihan — *Born Speaking Lies*
Colin Mitchell — *Roadman*
Ilan Mochari — *Zinsky the Obscure*
Gregory Papadoyiannis — *The Baby Jazz*
Andy Potok — *My Father's Keeper*
Robert Rosenberg — *Isles of the Blind*
Ron Savage — *Voyeur in Tangier*
David Schein — *The Adoption*
Fred Skolnik — *Rafi's World*
Lynn Sloan — *Principles of Navigation*
L.E. Smith — *The Consequence of Gesture*
L.E. Smith — *Travers' Inferno*
Bob Sommer — *A Great Fullness*
Tom Walker — *A Day in the Life*
Susan V. Weiss —*My God, What Have We Done?*
Peter M. Wheelwright — *As It Is On Earth*
Suzie Wizowaty — *The Return of Jason Green*

Poetry

Antonello Borra — *Alfabestiario*
Antonello Borra — *AlphaBetaBestiaro*
James Connolly — *Picking Up the Bodies*
Greg Delanty — *Loosestrife*
Mason Drukman — *Drawing on Life*

Fomite

Stories

Fomite

Andrei Guriuanu — *Body of Work*
Derek Furr — *Semitones*
Derek Furr — *Suite for Three Voices*
Zeke Jarvis — *In A Family Way*
Marjorie Maddox — *What She Was Saying*
William Marquess — *Boom-shacka-lacka*
Gary Miller — *Museum of the Americas*
Jennifer Anne Moses — *Visiting Hours*
Peter Nash — *Parsimony*
Martin Ott — *Interrogations*
Jack Pulaski — *Love's Labours*
Charles Rafferty — *Saturday Night at Magellan's*
Kathryn Roberts — *Companion Plants*
Ron Savage — *What We Do For Love*
L.E. Smith — *Views Cost Extra*
Caitlin Hamilton Summie — *To Lay To Rest Our Ghosts*
Susan Thomas — *Among Angelic Orders*
Tom Walker — *Signed Confessions*
Silas Dent Zobal — *The Inconvenience of the Wings*

Odd Birds

Micheal Breiner — *the way none of this happened*
David Ross Gunn — *Cautionary Chronicles*
Gail Holst-Warhaft — *The Fall of Athens*
Roger Leboitz — *A Guide to the Western Slopes and the Outlying Area*
dug Nap— *Artsy Fartsy*
Delia Bell Robinson — *A Shirtwaist Story*
Peter Schumann — *Planet Kasper, Volumes One and Two*
Peter Schumann — *Bread & Sentences*
Peter Schumann — *Faust 3*
Peter Schumann — *We*

Plays

Stephen Goldberg — *Screwed and Other Plays*
Michele Markarian — *Unborn Children of America*